The Love That Will Not Let Me Go

Heather {Stewart} Harris

ISBN: 145288451X
ISBN-13: 9781452884516

Introduction

"I am too proud! I am too proud!"

These were the only words that escaped from my mouth as I yelled at the top of my lungs. I finally felt confident enough to tell everyone in the hospital why the Lord was punishing me. I hoped by this realization and by exposing it to everyone that it would be the end to this horrifying nightmare that I was living.

With the very morsel strength that I had left I ripped the IV from my veins. Not giving it any thought as the needle shot out of my arm, and blood dripped to the floor. I didn't care what I had to do even if it caused me great pain. I had to do everything humanly possible to get to the hallway to let the nurses, doctors and my family know what separated me from God. I knew this inspiration was sent from God himself. He wanted me to let everyone know before my agony would end.

When I finally made my way to the hall the stress and anxiety that I experienced forced my feeble and fatigued body to collapse on the floor. As I blinked away the tears that filled my eyes I made out the familiar face of my father. I was so relieved that he was there to comfort me. It filled me with joy to see his face.

As I laid on the floor I stretched out my arms as if I was being nailed to the cross. The unexplainable bruises on both my wrist were exposed, and it really looked as if I had been nailed.

For the first time in several months I felt a little bit of relief. Had I finally figured out what separated me from God? Could our relationship be restored? Was it too late to be redeemed from hell?

Something suddenly happened again. As more and more nurses and people rushed to my side I started to get overwhelmed. The uncertainty caused stress to take over my body again. My heart pounded and vibrated throughout my body. Agonizing stabbing chest pains sent aches down my arm. I felt like someone had cut off my airway. I suddenly couldn't breathe, and I gasped for air. Stress had attacked me again.

As more and more people enveloped me I knew it was time to haul me off to the horrid place where I would be gruesomely tortured forever. I was headed for hell!

Where was God's love now, that love that would not let me go? I shamed him so much that he let me go, and I would suffer horrific pain forever. These thoughts ran through my head as I helplessly laid on the hospital floor. Even my own earthly father, who stood by my side, could not help me now. At this point everyone knew, except for me, that I definitely was not in my right mind.

Chapter • One

....

Our Godly Home

66 For I know the plans I have for you, declares the Lord, plans to prosper you and not to harm you, plans to give you hope and a future. 99

Jeremiah 29:11

As a child I was raised in a very loving and religious home. I can't remember a time when I didn't know the Lord.

God has blessed my siblings and me with wonderful parents, who love the Lord. Through their actions and words we could easily see that they had a faithful relationship with God. They wanted us to have the same relationship, and they encouraged us by making sure we went to church every Sunday. Sundays were set aside to honor our father in heaven.

A Sunday morning in our house would include waking up early, to get ready for church, or at least it seemed early to us. We never wanted to get up on Sunday mornings. It was our weekend to rest.

"This is not fair!" We would complain to Mom and Dad. "It is the weekend, and we want to sleep in!"

Growing up we did not appreciate the Sundays when our parents forced us out of bed so that we could attend another boring church service. We had to be deathly ill if we even thought about asking Mom and Dad to stay home from church.

One Sunday, our parents decided to take us on our yearly summer vacation to Six Flags. We couldn't believe that this happened on a Sunday. Bless our parents' hearts we had a Sunday school lesson in the back of our 1980 grey Station Wagon. We sang songs, listened to a Bible story and prayed. We praised the Lord as we drove to our vacation destination.

Our family was always involved with church. Our schedule was occupied with youth group, Bible School, church camp and Christmas programs. My mom dedicated her time for the Lord. She organized most of these events. Everyone in the church depended on Mom to step up and lead. She was one that could never say no.

I really admired my mom because she worked so hard and made every event at church a success. She would always out do herself and put on elaborate programs that impressed everyone. Her Bible School programs were always extraordinary. The creative decoration ideas that Mom would come up with would include palm trees, animals, murals and many other imaginative scenes that made the theme come to life.

My father is a very godly man, and his faith is revealed in everything that he does. As long as I have been living I have never heard a swear word come out of his mouth or even the Lord's name. No matter how much work needed to be done, on Sunday, he rested and read the Bible. He never spoke harshly about anyone even those who were unkind. My father sees the good in everyone, and I really admire him for that.

I can remember having family devotions in our living room. The whole family would learn about the Lord together. At the time, we were not too thrilled about spending our evenings this way. Now, I look back, and I'm glad we had devotions.

It helped us grow closer to God as a family. Dad would sit in his cozy recliner that was reserved only for him. Everyone except me squeezed on the couch to listen to Dad read from the Bible. I would warm myself in front of our fireplace during the chilly winter evenings. As I reminisce I can still feel the warmth of the fire as it comforted my frigid body. I loved to hear my father's soothing voice read God's word. We would pray, read and share God's love with each other. I cherish those memories with the family.

My parents would do anything for us. They worked hard to provide for our needs and they did the best they could to give us what we wanted. I know they struggled to make ends meet, but as children we did not realize this. I appreciate them for that, and I wish I had shown them more appreciation as I was growing up. The one thing that I thank them for the most is raising us to love the Lord. I truly respect them for that, and I will continue to raise my children the same way.

It is hard to believe that a child who was raised in this spiritual environment would face the horrific dilemma that I faced as an adult. How could I be so confused about my faith and not feel that I had the assurance of heaven? Now, I realize that our heavenly Father never promised a perfect life. A person will face dilemmas no matter what environment they are raised in, that way they may realize their total dependence on him. God is good even in the toughest situations. It might not seem like it during these tough times, but he works all things out for the good of those who love him.

Chapter • Two

···············

The Family Farm

"Therefore I tell you, do not worry about your life,
what you will eat or drink; or about your body, what
you will wear. Is not life more important than food, and
the body more important than clothes?**"**
Matthew 6:25

I have two loving sisters and a wonderful brother.
Mariah is my older sister who is only ten months
older. My youngest brother is David, and my precious baby sister is Megan.

I love my sisters and brother so much. We
have very close relationships. I know that they
would help me out with anything. We grew even
closer as we worked on our family farm. When
we were younger we felt forced against our will
to work on the farm, but looking back I realized
that the farm instilled the hard working character that all four of us have as adults. Honestly
I think all of us loved the farm, but we didn't
know it at the time. It helped us value our family
even more.

Megan was the fortunate baby sister who never had to endure the hard labor that Mariah, David, and I did as children. She was pardoned because she was the youngest. To this day we always give her a hard time about it, but we love her anyway. From following to close to a sick cow that showered her with diarrhea to falling into a manure pit, she kept life on the farm entertaining. These memories always bring laughter to our family's conversations.

There were the bitterly cold snowy evenings of milking cows. The stench of the kerosene heater still fills my nose on chilly winter nights. This heater was the only means of keeping warm in the below freezing barn as we helped Dad finish the work for another day. I would always huddle by the heater warming my hands and my body as I anxiously counted my 13 cows that I had to milk. I constantly curled my toes in my farm boots. Three pairs of socks did not even help them from freezing. I couldn't wait to run to the phone in the barn, and dial up the next lucky cow milker.

"David, it is your turn!" I would say with a little snicker.

We each had our own share of chores to do. My chores were to clean the milkers and the milk hoses. After they were cleaned and sanitized I would hang them in the milking parlor so the cows could be milked. We had to do our chores promptly at four o'clock after school. It was very hard to get motivated to do this especially after being at school all day. There were other chores that included feeding and watering the cows. Struggling to lift five gallon buckets of corn was very difficult, and I know for sure that was why wimpy little Heather never got that job. It was hard work, but it was good for us. It helped us learn responsibility and appreciate a hard earned dollar.

I also remember and cherish the memories that summer on the farm brought. The sweltering sun would beat down on us as we worked in the fields. Sweat would roll down our backs and drench our clothes as we loaded hay bales. I would volunteer to drive the tractor as everyone would throw the fifty pound bales onto the wagon. We were all drained at the end of the day from the excruciating heat and strenuous labor. Our family would retire to bed early after a long day of farm work.

I always anticipated Grandma and Grandpa Stewart coming home from Arizona during the summer. They lived right behind us, and as a little girl I loved to sit and wait on our hill as they drove up our lane. Our family welcomed them with open arms. My siblings and I spent precious time with our loving grandparents, and they will always have a special place in my heart when I reminisce about life on the farm. Every morning after we helped Dad clean the barn we strolled up to Grandma and Grandpa's house as we let the cows out to the pasture. Many times Grandma would have breakfast ready for us. I loved sinking my teeth into her delicious hot waffles with maple syrup. We would sit in their backyard smelling the sweet aroma of their beautiful pink peonies as we watched the cows stroll down to the pasture. Life on the farm was great until those dreaded Saturday mornings during the school year came around.

We hated Saturday mornings when we were awaken by the annoying ring of the phone. On the other end would be our loving father telling us it was time to come out and clean the barn.

One morning my true character was revealed when the phone rang. I was so mad that I had to get up on another Saturday morning. I knew it had to be the routine phone call of our dad.

"What do you want?" I furiously yelled.

I was embarrassed when I heard the sweet voice of my Aunt Joyce on the other end.

"Mariah?" she said.

That behavior was more of Mariah's character than timid little Heather's.

I transformed back to my usual quiet self and said I was sorry.

We were hard workers because our parents instilled this in us. Our parents knew that the Lord did not want us to become lazy. The farm was a blessing from the Lord. It brought our family together in many ways, and it helped us grow in Christ.

The Family Farm

This is the farm where I was born and raised. Our house is the first white house and Grandma and Grandpa Stewart's house is the trailer in the back of the picture. Many memories were made here as we worked hard in the barn and fields.

Mariah and I were very close. It is Easter morning, and we are ready for church. We could not wait to show off our beautiful dresses. We felt grown-up with our purses. We made a great pair.

The 4-H shows were always fun. David, Mariah and I en-joyed showing our calves so that we could win ribbons and money. These days were always hot, but we loved getting up early and staying at the fairground all day.

Summer days working in the fields were exhausting. David uses all of his strength as he loads the straw bale on the wagon. All of us worked hard to get the field work done for the day. Our loyal dog, Max, was always around to help out, too.

The Family Farm

This is the family. My sisters, brother, Mom, Dad and I. We have a special bond that can never be broken.

David's wedding was an exciting day. We were all happy for him and his new wife, Emma Carson. Megan wore the beautiful bridesmaid dress while Mariah and I read Bible verses during the service. It was a beautiful wedding.

Chapter Three

....

People-Pleaser

" Fear the Lord, you his saints, for those who fear him lack nothing... Come, my children, listen to me; I will teach you the fear of the Lord. **"**

Psalm 34:9, 11

People-pleaser is the perfect description that describes my personality. As long as I can remember I have struggled with being accepted by others, and I needed this acceptance to make me feel good about myself. The problem with this was that I have lived my life in total bondage. People have controlled me, and it has left me feeling empty. I feared man when I should have feared the Lord. I replaced God with people. While feeling that this sin was the reason why I suffered I soon realized that I suffered so that God could bring this sin to my attention and then help me change it.

I have always been shy and self-conscious. I always strived to be the perfect daughter, the perfect student, the perfect wife and the perfect mother. Not realizing it, this impossible goal that I had set for myself was creating a lot of stress and anxiety in my life. It was completely controlling every move and thought I made. I would constantly beat myself up when I made a mistake or caused someone to become upset at me. I wanted everyone to be happy, and I was not happy if they were not. I would lose sleep and worry over minor issues that most of the time I had no control over anyway. Besides this struggle, the Lord was trying to get my attention with other issues.

I committed my life to the Lord at the age of 9. I was at Church Camp when this transformation took place. The Holy Spirit moved me as I listened to the messages and as we praised the Lord with inspirational songs. I knew that this was supposed to be a life changing experience, but I didn't really feel any different at the time. Now that I received the Lord into my life, what happens next? I was still confused about this new life that I was supposed to live. I was a new Christian, and I had a long way to go to fully understand who I was as a child of God. With time, the Lord revealed the answers to some of my questions, but there was one question that terrified me. How did I really know that I was going to heaven when my life on earth was done? I did not have this assurance, and this also added to my stress and negatively affected my life. Would the Lord let me go if I continued to live my life fearing man? I thought I had to be perfect to get into heaven. My whole life I had always visualized God shaking his finger at me every time I sinned, and I thought that I had to continually ask the Lord back into my life. This seemed to be a never ending process and a hopeless resolution to a problem that seriously needed fixed.

On the surface my life seemed normal, and as a straight A student I was constantly told how fortunate I was to be a hard working goal oriented person. Everyone knew I would be successful because of my positive perspective of school and work. I knew that this perspective was definitely important to my future, but deep down I had an inner struggle that I fought with most of my life. My battle with being perfect affected my life in school, sports, and my career as an adult. I pressured myself so much that I did not enjoy my life. I did not take the time to relax and appreciate the little things in life.

As a student I studied four to five hours for tests. I forced myself to know every single word in my notes perfectly, and if I made anything less than an A on a test I would worry about my grade. I did not want my parents to be disappointed or ashamed of me. I worried about letting my teachers down. I had to get the scholarships, and I strived to get Valedictorian. I was not happy with myself unless I was perfectly successful at everything I did. I wanted to impress everyone and not let God or my family down. My perspective on life forced me to be uptight, and I missed the exciting experiences in life because I was too stressed to enjoy them. I created unnecessary anxiety in my life, and that caused me to worry much more than I needed. Most people thought that my success in school came easy, but my feelings toward life made it tough. I know I did not trust God during my life, and I failed to place my worries into his hands. I did not allow God to guide my life. I put myself in the driver's seat.

Sports were another issue that was negatively affected by my life of perfection and pride. I loved volleyball, but I was not very successful at it because I worried about what others thought of me. I did not have the confidence that I needed to play up to my potential. I could have been much better if I would have looked to the Lord for guidance and assurance. I was so nervous during games because I worried that I would make a mistake. I wanted to be accepted by my teammates, coach, and the fans. I knew I did not play up to my teammates' and coaches' expectations, and this made me feel worthless and disappointed in myself. I wanted to be the best setter, but I failed because of my personal struggle and failing to trust in the Lord.

As an adult, or at least until God opened my eyes and changed my perspective, I struggled with my career as a teacher. I almost gave my career up because of the stress that I created for myself in the classroom. I wanted to successfully change every child in my room. I wanted every student to read, write, and do math perfectly. If they didn't or they misbehaved I would blame myself. I would spend many evenings after school in tears because I felt like I was failing as a teacher. I did not take into consideration the lack of abilities and parent involvement in most of my students' lives. I wanted to change things that I had no control over. As I was growing up I longed to become a successful teacher but because of my perspective I hated my teaching job. I had to force myself to get out of bed to face another school day. I failed to take one day at a time, and I would worry about the next day before it even arrived. I hated my job and this needed to change.

I second-guessed all of my decisions because I feared what other people would think. I wanted to look perfect in the eyes of everyone and I was too proud for them to see my flaws. The Lord decided it was time to change this. As a Christian, God did not want me to live this way. He had to use a horrifying life changing psychological episode to get my attention. My personal awakening to this problem came during the summer of 2005.

Chapter • Four

....

The Beginning of a Personal Awakening

66 And this is the testimony: God has given us <u>eternal</u> life, and this life is in his Son. He who has the Son has life; he who does not have the Son of God does not have life. I write these things to you who believe in the name of the Son of God so that you may know that you have <u>eternal</u> life. 99

I John 5:11-12

I can remember it like it was just yesterday when my personal awakening started.

I had just ended a very long stressful year as a 1st grade teacher, and on top of that my husband, Will, and I had faced many marital problems. We struggled with the decision of separating. The stress and anxiety that came as I dealt with a very difficult school year and the issues with my marriage slowly deteriorated me physically and mentally.

It was a hot June day, and the sun pounded down on my body, which made me feel worse than I had ever felt. We were at my cousin's graduation party, and I didn't know what had happened to me. It didn't feel normal. Being the people pleaser that I was I did not want anyone to know that I felt very strange. I did not want to cause any problems or ruin my cousin's celebration day.

I did not have an appetite, and whenever I did eat it was very difficult just to swallow food. My stomach was in knots, and my chest ached with pain. My whole body felt drained and weak, and my head spun as the excruciating heat made it even more difficult. It was like my body experienced stress every minute of the day without any relief.

No one knew that I headed into the house to sit down. It was air-conditioned, and I hoped the cool air would give me some relief. I slowly sat down on the couch, and I tried not to move too fast. I sat with my eyes closed and prayed that I would feel better so that I could get back outside to enjoy my family.

Besides the symptoms that I experienced, I was also extremely tired because I could not sleep at night. Ever since I was very young I would have times when I could not sleep. The activities of the day would run through my brain. My mind was very active and I worried about the decisions I had to make. I often convinced myself that it was impossible for me to sleep and because of this I wouldn't. I actually believed that I was incapable of sleeping. I would become very frustrated, and the thought of not sleeping at night overwhelmed me and caused me great anxiety. Even as an adult my sleeping problem was worse. I had only nine hours of sleep in the past three days.

Feeling a little relieved I decided to return to the party. I slowly rose up from the couch but now I felt nauseated. When I stepped outside the pounding heat hit me like a brick wall. My head spun, and the sun blinded me. I finally made it over to Will, but I couldn't hide it anymore. Suddenly everything went black and my limp body fell to the ground.

I remembered that I opened my eyes, and everyone was huddled around me. They asked me how I felt and if they could help me inside. I was helped into the house and was laid on the bed. My precious girls, Hannah and Adrianna, rushed into the room, and by the look on their faces I could tell they were very worried. I touched both of their hands with a soft motherly touch, and I reassured them that Mommy was going to be fine.

There was a retired doctor at the party who asked me questions and gave me some advice. His major concern was that I did not sweat at all after I fainted. He said that I should have sweated profusely. He told me that I got over-heated. I was to make sure that I called my family physician first thing in the morning.

For some reason I was not truly convinced that this was the cause of my symptoms. I didn't know it, but this was just the beginning of a long summer of agony but absolutely an awakening from the Lord.

Chapter • Five

....

The 911 Call

" Do not be anxious about anything, but in everything by prayer and petition, with thanksgiving present your requests to God. And the peace of God, which transcends all understanding, will guard your hearts and your minds in Christ Jesus. **"**

Philippians 4:6 & 7

The next day I called to get an appointment with my family physician. I got in that day and told the doctor the symptoms that I experienced the day before. He also asked me about some of the stress that affected my life. My doctor gave me some advice on how to alleviate my daily stress. I was already on Wellbutrin, a medication for anxiety. I had been taking it a little over a year. The doctor did not want to increase the dosage because I was already taking a pretty high dose. His reasons why I fainted were because of the heat and the stress that I was under. I was told to try some of his stress alleviating ideas and to call for another appointment in a month.

A week had passed, and I had been feeling better. Will and I worked out our problems, and we decided that separating was not a good idea. I had also decided to stop taking the Wellbutrin because I had read that this medicine can cause sleeplessness, and I wanted to resolve that issue, too.

Everything seemed like it was back to normal, and we decided to take a trip to Holiday World in Santa Clause, Indiana. Hannah and Adrianna are always excited about going on this three hour trip to ride roller coasters and spend a hot summer day refreshed in the water park. We always drive to Santa Clause, go to Holiday World and then stay the night at a hotel. It is always great family fun that we all look forward to.

As we rushed out the door that June summer day I grabbed a hot dog to eat on the road. I gulped it down so fast I didn't even get time to taste it. After about two hours I started to feel very strange again. I felt as if the hot dog was stuck in my throat, and I could not breathe. Everything was extremely bright and my head ached. I kept it quiet for a while, but then I had to warn Will.

"Will! Will!" I said in a panicked voice. "I cannot breathe. I think I am choking on my hot dog!"

"You can't be choking you ate it over two hours ago, and you are talking." He said without any concern.

"Call 911! Please Call 911! I'm going to faint and I can't hang on any longer!" I yelled as I breathed heavy and gasped for air.

"Are you serious?" he said with more concern.

Will fumbled for his cell phone and became very nervous as I started to cry.

"Mommy! Mommy! What is wrong?" Adrianna said with a tear in her eye. "Are you sick again?"

I was so upset that I could not answer her. All I could do was cry. Will was on the phone, and he tried to stay calm as he got directions to the nearest hospital. I tried my best to hang on, but it was very difficult. I felt very faint. My chest felt very heavy, and my breathing was not normal.

Will drove at a very high speed. He got off at the nearest exit and looked for the blue hospital signs. He followed them, and he finally found the hospital. It felt like it took forever. To my surprise I was still conscious.

We pulled up to the emergency room door, and a nurse came out with a wheelchair. She helped me out of the van. As she wheeled me into the hospital I noticed that the doctors and nurses were very calm, and they did not act like it was a life-threatening emergency. This really relieved my anxiety, and I breathed normally again.

They took me to a bed, but I still felt very strange. The nurse took my vitals and asked me a few questions. She left me by myself in the room for about ten minutes. During those ten minutes I talked to the Lord. I said this little prayer.

"Lord if there is anything that I have done to cause you to become angry with me I am truly sorry. I love my family so much, and I would really like to enjoy them during this trip. Please help me to feel better so I can serve you and enjoy what you have blessed me with."

I opened my eyes and my precious family stood in the room with me. My wonderful girls came to my side, and I hugged and kissed them. Will leaned over and hugged me and asked me how I was doing. Shortly after that a nurse came in with some medicine for my anxiety. The doctor came in right behind the nurse. He asked me if I was on any medication for my anxiety. I told the doctor about the Wellbutrin that I was on, and I had stopped taking it because I thought that it caused my sleepless nights. A really worried look suddenly covered his face, and with great concern he said that was the problem. He told me that I could not stop taking an antidepressant like that. The doctor must slowly wean the patient off of this medicine. He knew for sure that the side effects were the direct result of me suddenly stopping my medication. He told me to make sure I called my family physician, and tell him what had happened.

The doctor wrote me a prescription for the Wellbutrin. I had not been off of it very long so he said the best thing would be to get back on it, and then ask my doctor about weaning me off of it. The doctor kept me until I was feeling better, and he said it was perfectly fine to go to Holiday World. He told me to make sure that I drink plenty of water and to rest when I felt like I needed to.

About two hours later we left, and we were headed to Holiday World. We stopped at the nearest pharmacy to pick up the Welbutrin prescription. I started the medicine again, and I felt better. Our trip was fun, and we got home safely without anymore 911 calls.

It wasn't until a couple of days after we got back when my family and I started to really worry. I started to experience more symptoms, but these were strange psychological symptoms that eventually forced me to become institutionalized. I questioned my faith and I feared that God had let me go. I was truly convinced that my hopeless fate was hell!

Chapter • Six

....

Evil Glares

❝Cast all your anxiety on him because he cares for you.**❞**

I Peter 5:7

Evil glares cut through me like daggers as I cautiously walked into Wal-Mart. I felt as if everyone stared at me. They seemed to know that something eccentric was happening in my life. I felt like my psychological problems had been made known to everyone.

Eyes stared at me as if they analyzed my every thought. Some stares seemed like they were from concerned parents who tried to steer their children away from me. The constant glare of what seemed like every eye watching me made me overwhelmed, and I left Wal-Mart crying. I was so stressed I did not buy anything. I was terrified by this event, and I felt like I had gone crazy. I headed home to tell Will.

"Will, they were all glaring at me! They know everything about me and I am scared!" I said in a panicked voice.

This disturbed me, and I could hardly breathe. My hands sweated, and I gasped for air after every word. My whole body shook as if I had seen a ghost.

Will lovingly put a hand on my shoulder and told me to take a deep breath and calm down.

"Who was glaring at you?" He asked with a very confused look.

Finally, after I calmed down I was able to explain what happened in Wal-Mart.

My husband reassured me that people were not staring at me, and there was no way they could know about my problems.

Then he mentioned, for the first time, taking me to the hospital.

This scared me even more. What would they do to me? What would happen to me? The horrifying scenes from psychological movie overwhelmed my mind. I thought of the scenes where the main character is crazy and is forced into an insane asylum. The treatment is dreadful. I had to hold back my tears as I thought about it.

I told Will that I would be fine, and I did not want to go to the hospital even though I knew the worst was yet to come.

Chapter • Seven

·····························

Sleepless Nights

"In vain you will rise early and stay up late, toiling for food to eat- for he grants sleep to those he loves.**"**

Psalm 127:2

The mind is a powerful thing. It can literally convince the body that it is not capable of sleep. That is what happened to me during that summer of 2005.

I was exhausted almost to death. It is a feeling that is very difficult to explain. My body felt like it was asleep, but my mind would not rest. My eyes would be wide open, and my brain would be going a hundred miles a minute. I couldn't feel my body as I lay in bed night after night. It frustrated me, and the more frustrated I got the more my mind would race.

"What if I'm not capable of sleeping? What if I never sleep again?" These questions filled my thoughts, and I actually believed that I couldn't sleep.

I was averaging about two hours a night and some nights I didn't get any sleep at all. This went on for about two months.

I dreaded nighttime when it was time to sleep. It was stressful to me because I knew another sleepless night was yet to come. My whole day was filled with thoughts about sleeping. I could not concentrate on anything else. It consumed my life. This was the stress that I endured; it devoured my life and made me feel as far away from God as possible.

This stress affected me so much that I decided to turn to the Bible, but the devil was at work. I misinterpreted what the Lord wanted me to see. The devil prowled throughout the whole summer. He tried to destroy my life and my faith. I read the Bible and thought that I did not sleep because it was part of the Lord's punishment. I was convinced that this was the chastisement that I experienced because I continued to sin. My sin was the fear of man and being so proud that I had to look and act perfect in the presence of everyone.

The devil had convinced me that the Lord had left me behind to fend for myself.

Tears filled my eyes, as I felt hopeless lying in my bed. I listened to the quietness of the house. At exactly 2:00 every morning I sat with my girls while they slept. I took Adrianna's hand and sat by her bed while she slept soundly. It was actually the only thing that relaxed me at night because I knew that my precious girls were getting their sleep. Then I would go to Hannah's room and do the same. I wanted to be as close to my girls as possible because I did not know what was going to happen to me. I had a feeling that I would be without my girls for a while.

Chapter • Eight

....

Hearing Voices

66I will lie down and sleep in peace, for you alone,
O Lord, make me dwell in safety. **99**

Psalm 4:8

Hearing voices was one of the most terrifying
and mentally exhausting symptom that occurred
during my mental illness. It was literally a war
between good and evil, and I was caught in the
middle. I heard what I thought was the voice of
God and the voice of the Devil.

These voices came suddenly while I stared
in the darkness losing another night's sleep.
I faintly remember what was said the first time
I heard these sounds. I just remember being so
terrified that my heart raced, and every muscle
in my body tensed. It was as if I awoke from the
most frightening nightmare, but I cried knowing that I never went to sleep. This was my reality
that I could not escape.

Both voices sounded exactly the same, but they obviously served different purposes. There was no inflection or feeling in either. Their voices were very monotone and very disturbing. I heard these sounds at nighttime when I was the most frustrated and could not sleep.

The voice that I recognized as Satan's always filled my head with dark terrifying thoughts. He only spoke brief sentences such as:

"You're headed for Hell!" or "You're living in sin!"

I never talked back or held a conversation with this voice. I broke down and cried when I heard it because I seriously believed all the devious lies that came from this voice. I covered my ears and refused to listen, but it didn't work. These influential words haunted me, and they became very real.

The voice that I thought was God's was different. When I heard this voice I wanted to talk back and hold a conversation with it. I wanted to grab on to it and not let go.

The best way that I can explain this feeling is when you finally receive a phone call from a loved one who is miles away, and you never want to hang up. It is a phone call that you long for because you never know when they are going to call back. It leaves an ache in your heart that never goes away.

Every time God's voice left I felt further and further away from him as if he left me and was never coming back. I felt hopeless and alone.

As I look back I truly do not believe God or Satan was actually talking to me. I do believe that it was my mind making me believe that my own thoughts were these voices. It was just a symptom caused by my mental illness.

Chapter • Nine

·····················

Too Much to Handle

"Jesus said-"I tell you the truth, he who believes has
everlasting life."**"**

John 6:47

I stared intently at my wrists as I noticed bruises.
They suddenly appeared, and I had no idea
where they came from. I started to panic as
I frantically tried to rub the bruises off. I rubbed
and rubbed as hard as I could but they did not
disappear. I was bothered with the fact that I did
not know why these bruises were on me. Then
I finally thought I had the answer.

"I have been marked!"

Everyone would know who I am. They would
know me as the one who claimed to be a child
of God but continued to live in sin. With this
thought in mind I rubbed even harder. It was
hopeless just like everything else in my life.

As each day passed life got harder to handle.
I started to interpret everything differently. Every

time I looked in the mirror I saw a pathetic hideous demonic figure. I tried to avoid looking in any mirror because it depressed me even more. I had dark circles under my eyes from the lack of sleep. I felt the weight of depression, and it was easily seen in the way I dressed and the way I looked. I felt like there was no point in fixing myself up. Life was hopeless for me and I was alone. I was truly convinced that I had no hope of heaven.

My mind could not grasp how hot hell would actually be. I had to know since that was where I was going to spend eternity. It was as if I had accepted my eternal fate, and I tried to prepare myself for what was to come. I decided to turn on the oven to see if I could handle the heat. When the burner was heated to high I placed my hand as close to it as I could without touching it. I wanted to see how long I could hold my hand above the heat. The heat was so intense on my hand I was only able to hold it there for about five seconds. I dropped to the floor and cried. I raised my hands to the heavens, and I cried out to the Lord.

"Have mercy on me Lord! I won't be able to handle the intense heat on my body for eternity!"

I laid on the floor, and tears rolled down my face. I felt hopeless because I knew that the Lord did not hear my cry for help. He was gone and I was on my own to withstand my severe punishment forever.

Chapter • Ten

....

A Cry for Help

"O Lord hear my prayer, listen to my cry for mercy; in your faithfulness and righteousness come to my relief. **"**

Psalm 143:1

My family realized that it was time to seek help.

It was another hot summer day in June, and my mom and dad came to our house to swim. I tried to hide the fact that I was mentally confused and severely depressed. My parents asked me how I was doing, but I lied and told them that I felt much better. I know that they were not convinced.

My mom noticed how tired I was and told me to lie down and rest. I decided that if I took a nap it would be the best thing.

I laid in my bed just as I did at night. I stared at the ceiling without a wink of sleep. Suddenly I heard the voice again.

"It is time for you to die!"

The voice that I dreaded to hear haunted my thoughts with these words. The sound of these words suddenly overwhelmed my body with stress. My heart raced and my stomach churned. If these words were correct I knew where I was headed.

I slowly got out of bed, but I could hardly stand. I felt like I was going to faint, and I thought that this was death taking over my body.

I frantically yelled for Will, Mom, and Dad. I went outside and told them that I felt very strange, and I was dying.

My mom jumped out of the pool and comforted me. The rest of my family was right behind her. She sat me down and took my pulse. My pulse raced.

"You've lost hope," my mom said with tears in her eyes.

I shook my head yes and held on to my girls' hands. I told them that I loved them very much.

My family helped get my feeble body to the couch. I laid there convinced that I only had a few minutes left of my life.

Will called for an ambulance and we waited patiently for it to arrive. It seemed like forever before it got to our house. Every minute that it took I felt like my thoughts became more demonic. I glanced around the room and noticed that the faces in our family pictures looked dark and demon like. Something unexplainable forced me to glare into everyone's eyes as if I were coaxing them to the dark side. I was aware that it made everyone uncomfortable especially the EMT crew. It didn't bother me, and I felt forced to continue.

New uncanny thoughts entered my corrupt mind. I felt that everyone was against me even my family. When I arrived at the hospital I knew the nurses and the doctors were in on the plan to send me to my eternal destination.

When I arrived at the hospital I was completely confused. My surroundings were unfamiliar to me. I didn't have the slightest idea where I was.

No one was on my side, and I had this uncontrollable urge to retaliate. I felt aggression boiling in my blood and being a very nonaggressive person this really felt strange to me. I had the mindset that I had to resist any type of force that was placed on me. I had no choice if I wanted to survive.

I was very uncooperative because in my mind everyone was my enemy. I refused everything from answering questions to eating and drinking. I didn't want any help from anyone.

The ER doctor came to the ridiculous conclusion that I was either on drugs or that I was faking. After the drug test came back negative the doctor told my family that I was faking to get attention. My family thought this was absurd.

"This is not like her!" My husband tried to explain.

"You don't know my wife! She is a first grade teacher and a loving mother of two girls."

My family demanded that I stay overnight. Even though he had a petulant attitude and acted like I was in the way he decided to keep me for observation.

I was not allowed to get out of bed. The hospital staff feared that I would hurt myself or someone else. The nurse inserted a catheter and an IV for fluids. After a long strenuous fight the nurses finally got the catheter and IV in place.

It was about thirty minutes later when I surprised everyone in the room. With all of my strength I pulled my catheter completely out.

"How did you do that without feeling any pain?" My mom commented with a perplexed look on her face.

I definitely did not make life easy for the hospital staff that night.

Chapter • Eleven

A Thief in the Night

66For you know very well that the day of the Lord
will come like a thief in the night.99

I Thessalonians 5:2

The horrendous racket of moaning and groan-
ing from other patients echoed in my ears.
I wanted the noise to stop so badly. The clamor
distracted my attention so much that it took me
awhile, but I realized I was by myself. It was very
dark.

"Where am I? What is going on?" I chanted
silently in my mind. I was panic-stricken.

The scene created horrific thoughts and
images in my head.

The Lord had come like a thief in the night
just as the Bible had said. I was by myself without
my family. I knew that Matthew 24:40-41 had
come true.

Two men will be in the field; one will be taken and the other left. Two women will be grinding with a hand mill; one will be taken and the other left.

I was left on Earth to perish in the end of age. My family was taken by the Lord to enjoy the glory and peace of heaven for eternity. I would never see my precious girls or hear their sweet voices again. There would be no more popcorn, hot chocolate, or movies at bedtime. I suddenly longed so much to hold them. I longed for it so much that there was a pain in my chest and a tear in my eye. There was nothing I could do to bring them or my wonderful husband back to me.

While I cried and reminisced about all of the wonderful memories my family and I shared, the light to my hospital room turned on. To my surprise my husband walked in with another doctor. It was hard to resist jumping out of bed to hug him, but I was attached to my IV. My smile stretched from ear to ear, and for that moment everything seemed wonderful. My husband was not gone, and I asked him questions about my mom, dad, and the girls. They were all fine and still on Earth with me. The Lord had not taken them away. If my precious girls had been there the moment would have been perfect.

Suddenly I felt offended and violated when Will and the doctor sat down and started to ask me questions.

"How could my husband share this personal information with another doctor?" I thought to myself.

I was very perturbed, and I drastically turned from being cooperative to being very stubborn.

The doctor asked questions about the voices I heard, how I felt, and if I felt like I wanted to hurt myself. I refused to answer, and I wanted both of them to leave. They were against me, and they wanted to get as much information from me as they could so they could send me away forever.

I drastically changed from one mood to another, and it exhausted me. Without any warning my attitude switched, and I knew this exhausted my family also.

They realized that I was not going to answer any questions or accept any food or water so they both left. I was alone in the dark to create new thoughts that ultimately caused my life to become even more difficult. I knew at this point that I was in for another sleepless night.

As I was trapped in the hospital I thought about what separated me from God.

"There has got to be something that I can do! Lord, show me the reason why you have left me behind! Bring me to this realization so that I can confess my sin." This was my conversation I had with God most of the night.

Suddenly my thoughts were interrupted when I realized what separated me from the Lord.

Pride! That was it! Pride was my greatest sin! My whole life I strived to be perfect because I was too proud to reveal my flaws. I wanted to please people, and I worked hard to gain their acceptance.

I had to let everyone know about this inspiration that was sent from God. I had to get to the hall to tell everyone. Maybe this would end my agony and put me on the right track with God.

"I am too proud! I am too proud!" These were the words that echoed through the hospital hallway early that morning.

Everyone needed to hear me to make them understand why I suffered.

I let everyone know this information, and it helped for a few minutes. Suddenly I felt uncertain and very frantic. My loving father stood at my side, and from the look on his face I knew he felt hopeless. At this point everyone knew, except for me, that I definitely was not in my right mind.

It felt like an angry mob surrounded me as nurses and my family ran to my side. I caused such a peculiar scene that it forced other patients to stare at the uncertainty of my behavior. The nurses and my family helped and cared for me, but I interpreted them as a threat

I gave the hospital staff such a terrible fight as they tried to get me off the floor and into a wheelchair. They finally wheeled me into a room by myself behind the nurses' desk. This is when

I had my first traumatic break down. I felt an uncontrollable rage to defend myself. I stopped at nothing to become free from the grips of hell.

"You're the devil! You're the devil!" I screamed at some of the staff.

My arms flew frantically in the air, and I hoped that they would defend me against the firm hold that everyone had on me. I chanted and screamed like a small child having a temper tantrum. When I seen a needle waved in my direction I knew I had to hurt someone to survive. As the nurse came closer and closer with the needle, without hesitation, I opened my mouth and gripped her arm so hard with my teeth that I drew blood. I was suddenly caught off guard when an extremely strong arm forced my neck and head into the pillow. I could not move as my arms and legs were restrained to the bed. I felt a sudden poke from the needle and my eyes gradually closed finally freeing my body and my mind from stress. I quickly drifted off to a much-needed sleep where I eventually awoke to unfamiliar surroundings.

Chapter • Twelve

Institutionalized

❝I have loved you with an <u>*everlasting love*</u>.**❞**
Jeremiah 31:3

"Is my nightmare over? Am I in the comfort of my own bed?"

These were the questions that I asked myself as my eyes gradually opened, but I was very disappointed as I glanced around the room and realized that my surroundings were unfamiliar to me.

"Where was I, and where was my family?"

Without moving a muscle I laid in my bed feeling completely confused. I slowly started to move my arms, feet, and neck, but my whole body ached. I felt like I had been in a fight. With this thought I was reminded about the biting incident at the hospital and how rough the nurses were with me when this happened. My jaw and neck ached so bad that it was painful to open my mouth or turn my head in either direction. I was then reminded of the strong force that threw my neck and face into the pil-low, and that was the last thing I remembered before I drifted off to sleep.

I was suddenly jolted out of my train of thought by the sounds of yelling and scream-ing. With the noise, confusion, and uncertainty I cried. I wanted to embrace my husband and my children and never let go, but that was impossible at this point.

I glanced around the room, and to my sur-prise I had a roommate. She was fast asleep in the bed right next to me. I started to wonder about the reason why she was there. I hoped that she was nice and we could become friends. Maybe she was experiencing the same symptoms, and we could actually relate to each other. I thought it would be nice to have a friend.

"Shower time! Shower time!" This echoed through the halls as the nurses were trying to get patients who wanted to take a shower.

I thought a shower would be nice. I would feel clean, relaxed, and ready to face the day, night or whatever time it was. I had no idea the time of day.

"Where are my clothes, my shampoo, or my soap? How was I supposed to take a shower without these things?"

I decided to get out of bed to find out where my things were. I sat up slowly and with caution I put my feet on the floor. I didn't want to get up too fast because I felt light headed and a little wobbly, but I did feel much better because I had slept. When I finally got to my feet I cautiously walked to the hall. I looked around like a lost child. I peered around the corner and suddenly felt out of place. The hallway felt cold and threatening as I timidly walked to the nurses' desk. It seemed like a mile long as everyone seemed to glare at me and asked me questions. There were no decorative pictures on the wall and I remembered it being dark and desolate. When I finally reached the nurses' desk I was almost afraid to talk.

"Where are my clothes, shampoo, and soap?" I said very timidly.

"What is your name?" the nurse asked.

"My name is Heather Harris?" I replied.

Without saying a word she gave me two bags. One bag had a familiar change of clothes and the other had soap and shampoo.

"Did my husband leave these clothes for me?" I asked curiously.

The nurse nodded "yes' and then turned to help another patient.

I turned to face the hall again. I did not know where the shower was so I decided to follow a few women who carried bags. We headed into the shower room and my stomach and mouth dropped when I seen that there were no doors on the showers or toilet stalls. There was absolutely no privacy as the nurses watched us shower and change. I was horrified when I realized I had to undress in front of everyone. I wondered how long I had to stay here.

I got through the very stressful shower, and I was extremely embarrassed. All I wanted to do was crawl back into bed and go to sleep. I actually felt like I could drift back to sleep. If I did I could get away from this awful and unfriendly place. That was exactly what I did, and sleep felt very nice.

Chapter • Thirteen

A Loving Visitor

> **❝**I tell you the truth; he who believes has _everlasting life_. **❞**
> John 6:47

I awoke to the sound of a familiar voice. I heard Will in the hallway talking to the nurses. I wanted to yell his name so bad, but I decided to wait for him to come into my room. After waiting for ten minutes I decided to jump out of bed to try to find him. The hall did not seem as threatening this time because I was focused on a mission to find my loving visitor.

I turned the corner and my husband was sitting at the table talking to a nurse. I couldn't resist. I hugged him. I did not want to let go because he made everything feel like it was going to be just fine. I wanted to talk to him and tell him how much I wanted to come home. The nurse left, and we sat and talked. I had so many questions to ask him.

"Do I get to go home? I really want to go home!"
I pleaded

"No, not yet, but I am working on getting you home as soon as possible." He said with regret.

"What is the problem? Where am I at?" I asked curiously.

Will explained the situation to me. He told me that I was on a psychiatric floor in a hospital in East St. Louis. I was placed in this hospital as opposed to a hospital closer to our home because it was the only hospital that would accept psychiatric patients who were unable to sign themselves in. I was not mentally stable enough to sign myself into another hospital. I was assigned a psychiatrist from the hospital, and I could not leave until he evaluated me. It was Saturday so there was no way to be evaluated until Monday. Will told me that he did some thinking and researched Welbutrin. He thought for sure that I had an allergic reaction to it because I kept getting on and off of the medicine. He said he thought the medicine was giving me psychological side effects. Will called our family physician, and he agreed. Will hoped that this would be enough of an evaluation to get me out of East St. Louis that day. He tried to get in contact with the psychiatrist from the hospital, and Will worked with the nurses to get in contact with him. They did not have much luck. A tear formed in my eye because I did not have hope that I was going home that day.

I told Will that I felt much better, and I felt like I was ready to go home. I wanted to see my wonderful children so that I could hold them and tell them how much I loved them. He reassured me that it would be soon, but I wanted the soon to be right then.

Will left me some magazines and books to read. It helped pass the time. He also left some snacks. I was very grateful that he brought these gifts. It was very painful to see him leave especially when I did not know exactly when he would be back to take me home. My husband returned home, and I was left in a cold and unfriendly environment where I struggled to have the patience to get through every minute of the day.

I sullenly walked back to my room and decided that I would sit on my bed and read. My roommate still slept so talking and making friends with her was out of the question. I was desperate, lonely, and needed my family. I prayed to the Lord that I would be able to go home soon. The emptiness in my heart was so strong that I felt like depression was attacking my thoughts.

An unpleasant yelling could be heard throughout the hall. The nurses rounded patients up, like cattle, to eat lunch. They sounded so petulant and unfriendly.

I actually felt like eating food so I willingly went up to the nurse and got my tray.

"What is your name?" She said rudely. She acted like I was in her way, and I took up her time.

I told her my name, and she handed me my tray without saying hi or asking me how I was doing. I slowly crept into the dining area, but I did not know where to sit. The dining area intimidated me because it was filled with peculiar patients. I did not know how to respond or act around some of them. Some patients stared, moaned and groaned, and others asked me inappropriate questions. A male in a wheelchair followed me around and made sexual comments toward me. I was very uncomfortable and needed the Lord more than anything at that point. I said a prayer before I ate, and I thought clearly now. It was torturous to be a sane person trapped in an insane world. I was actually in my right mind and feeling normal. I was eager to go home.

I looked for my roommate, but I did not see her at lunch. I finished my lunch and went straight to my room and got away from the bothersome patients that made me extremely uncomfortable. I wanted to tell my roommate that it was time to eat. To my surprise she awoke and sat on her bed.

"Hi! How are you doing?" I asked politely.

There was no response. She acted like I was not even there. She ignored me as if she were mad that I had spoken to her. She left the room, and I cried because I was alone and felt a great deal of discomfort. I wanted my family, and it was very hard to accept the fact that I would have to stay overnight.

Chapter • Fourteen

The Lord Answers

"My comfort in my suffering is this: Your promise preserves my life.**"**

Psalm 119:50

My eyes opened the next morning, and the greatest answer to prayer walked into my room. I was deeply grateful for the Lord's gracious answer.

"You're going home!" My husband yelled with excitement.

I jumped out of my bed and gave him the biggest hug I could possibly give. I did not want to let go. Everything seemed perfect and back to normal. I hadn't seen my precious girls in five days, and it felt like an eternity. I was eager to see their sweet smiles and hear their loving voices.

Around the corner came Aunt Sue and Grandma. They had come to see me home, and I was very happy to see family. It was such a relief to know that I was headed home, and I would not be tormented by other patients or be embarrassed by dreaded showers again.

The fresh air felt astonishing as I savored every breath. I stepped outside, and it was such a relief. I felt like I had been freed from my shackles. I was full of life, and the warmth of the bright sun refreshed me. I enjoyed the beauty of that wonderful June morning. That was the most remarkable day that I had had in a long time, but without my knowledge the worst was yet to come. My personal wakening was not even close to being over.

Chapter • Fifteen

A Party to Plan

" Trust in the Lord with all your heart and lean not on your own understandings. **"**

Proverbs 3:5

The heart-warming welcome that I received from Hannah and Adrianna was every mother's dream. It comforted me to know that they were well and I was actually home with them.

"You're home just in time for my birthday party!" Hannah yelled with excitement.

With all the commotion and being in and out of hospitals it had totally slipped my mind that we had planned a party for Hannah's birthday. The party was in just six days.

"Sweetie, I don't know if mommy will feel like having a party. We might have to wait and have your party later when mommy is feeling better," Will explained.

Her sweet smile and enthusiasm instantly disappeared. She had been looking forward to her party for several months. I couldn't stand to see her so sad, and I didn't want to let her down.

"No, we're having a party!" I said with confidence.

Hannah's face lit up with a beautiful smile, and she gave me the biggest hug that I had longed for for several days. My spirits were high, and I wanted my life back to normal again. I looked forward to having the party. I wanted to make this party the best one she ever had.

I knew I had a lot to plan before the party on Saturday. I had to order the cake, buy decorations, find a gift for Hannah and clean the house. I knew it was crucial that I put all my troubles behind me and focus on my daughter's birthday. I was very confident about this at the beginning of the week, but as the days went by my confidence declined. Negative thoughts started stirring up in my mind. I started to worry about sleeping again, and I fretted over being hospitalized. The more I worried the more my symptoms reoccurred as a result from my stress. It was a vicious cycle that I could not seem to get rid of.

I had to be strong for my daughter because I did not want to ruin her birthday. I tried my best to keep a clear mind. This was very difficult because the devastation of my hospital stay clouded my mind like a dark and gloomy day. I did not want hospitalization to become a reality again.

The day of Hannah's birthday party had arrived. The stress from the planning and organizing caught up with me. She invited about ten friends, and they were going swimming in our pool. It was about two hours before the party, and I started to have second thoughts about having it.

"Could I handle all these extra children with the stress that I was feeling?" I thought to myself.

I wasn't feeling up to it, but I forced myself. I kept going.

My mom arrived, and she was more than willing to help. She had that motherly sense that I would need her assistance. What a blessing it was to have her there. The preacher's wife, Jeanie Stark graciously volunteered to help also.

The party would not have been a success without their help.

The children started to arrive, and I wanted to enjoy the day. My mind was somewhere else. I watched everyone swim especially my two girls. They swam without a care in the world. They laughed and played as if there was nothing to worry about. A tear came to my eye as I thought about how much I loved them and how much they would be crushed if I had to return to the hospital. I wasn't back to normal and I knew it.

I tried to keep a smile on my face like nothing bothered me. I did not want anyone to worry. My mom told me to sit down and relax. She reassured me that Jeanie and her could handle the party.

"When is my life going to be normal again?" How much more will I be able to take? Lord, I know it says in your word that you will never give me more than what I can handle.

My oldest daughter turned six, and my mind was so distracted that I could not enjoy the day with her.

The stress of the party debilitated me and I felt like I needed to sleep. My mom and Jeanie helped me clean up the party. My mom offered to take my girls so that I could lie down. I was relieved and thankful for this offer. I wanted to sleep, but I had a feeling that I would not be able to. I took advantage of the quiet time and I tried to take a nap.

Chapter • Sixteen

Tragedy Returns

66 I have loved you with an *everlasting love*; I have drawn you with loving-kindness. **99**

Jeremiah 31:3

My plans for a relaxing nap failed because my tragic symptoms started again. The troubling voices snatched my attention, and it put me into disorder. The voices were bothersome, and I tried to ignore them. It was impossible. I screamed with pure terror and wept because I knew my tragedy had returned.

"Why?" I yelled. "Why me?"

I knew what I was in for. In a short time my perspective would be distorted. Everyone would be against me, and I would be alone to fight the entrapment of hell. Sleepless nights were ahead of me, and I did not want to face them.

I tried to sit down to watch T.V. to relax my mind, but it made the situation worse. It was very peculiar because I interpreted the T.V.

differently. Everything seemed to be directed toward me. It was as devastating as the voices that I heard. I suddenly realized that there was no escape. My mental illness devoured my life like a vicious lion.

Where was I to turn? Who was I to seek for help? This had to be something about my sinful nature. I wanted to make things right with God. I decided to read the Bible for answers. I looked up *sinning* in the index of my Bible to see if it would direct me to a verse that would help me. What I found devastated me. The index led me to this verse.

If you deliberately keep on sinning after we have received the knowledge of the truth, no sacrifice for sins is left, but only a fearful expectation of judgment and of raging fire that will consume the enemies of God. Hebrews 10:26-27

This verse confirmed my thinking, and I shook with fear. It was true that I was going to be consumed by raging fire. My nightmare had returned. It was too late to seek God's help because I was an enemy of God.

Obviously I had taken this verse out of context, and I had only interpreted a piece of the big picture. This verse is only referring to those who purposely shun God and turn from him. A Christian will still sin, but on their journey through life they will gradually turn from sin and eventually become more like Jesus, who was without sin. It is not until heaven will we be perfect, but God sees his children as perfect now. It is not what we do it is what Christ did for us on the cross. It is by God's grace not by our works. This is clearly explained in Ephesians 2:8-9

For it is by grace you have been saved, through faith and this is not from yourselves, it is a gift of God not by works so that no one can boast.

Suddenly, the phone startled me. I answered it, and it was my mom. She told me that Hannah and Adrianna wanted to stay the night, and she would come down to get their clothes. I did not tell her that I felt strange again. I didn't want her to worry, and I definitely did not want to go back to the hospital. She did ask me if I had slept, and I lied and told her that I just got up from a refreshing nap. There was no way that I could keep my mental illness a secret for very long. My husband would be home at 9:30 P.M. from work, and I knew he would ask me questions. He would see right through my strange behavior so I decided that I would have to act like I was sleeping when he got home.

I tried relaxing in a soothing bubble bath, but that did not help. My thoughts raced so bad that I could not keep up with them. I was going to explode from the stress that crippled my body. I knew I had to get into bed soon because Will would be home. I did not want to talk about my day, or tell him about my horrible experiences. How was I going to settle myself down in order to get into bed? I knew I had to prepare myself for the worst because sleep and relaxation was out of the question for the night. I sobbed with sorrow because I knew my situation was hopeless.

I heard the familiar sound of Will's car as he drove up our lane, but I was still crying. I had to keep it quiet so I could trick him into believing that everything was fine. He quietly walked into the room and gave me a loving kiss on my cheek, but I did not move. It was difficult to hold back the tears at this point because I knew my life with him was never going to be the same. I was going to be a prisoner to this disease forever. That was when this detrimental question tantalized my thoughts.

"Is it worth living my pathetic and mentally exhausting life anymore?"

I never dreamed that I would have suicidal thoughts, but I was being forced against my will to give up on my own life. I thought about how I could end my life, and this frightened me. At that point I didn't feel like I would follow through with it. I made plans, and that was the first sign of trouble. I cried the whole night from fear and depression. I tried many activities and hoped that I would fall asleep. I took a bath, read the Bible, listened to music, and watched T.V., but nothing was successful.

Morning finally arrived, and I was exhausted. I did not get any sleep, and I did not know how I was going to function. I didn't feel like doing anything. Cleaning the house, making breakfast and taking a shower were chores that I really needed to take care of, but I did not have the motivation to accomplish them.

Will had gone into town to get a few groceries so I was alone again to contemplate my troubles. What was I going to tell Will? I knew he was going to ask how I slept and how I felt. There was no way around it I had to tell him, but I knew I had to refuse to go to the hospital. I would not go back to that horrid place again.

The longer he was gone the weirder I felt. Visions of hell came to my mind again. I wanted to run away and never come back because I knew my husband would force me into my eternal destination. My whole family would turn on me, and I would be alone to fight for myself. The vicious cycle started again, and I knew I could not handle it anymore. I have to leave, but I was too late. Will walked in the house. How was I going to get by him?

Chapter • Seventeen

The Fight of My Life

66 May our Lord Jesus Christ himself and God our father, who loved us and by his grace gave us _eternal_ encouragement and good hope. 99

2 Thessalonians 2:16

Will obstructed the doorway so that I could not get out. I fought him with all my strength and I pleaded with him to let me go. I kicked and yelled because I had to get away. I told him that I did not want to go to the hospital, and I needed to leave.

"I have to take you to the hospital, and you do not have a choice!" Will tried to explain, but I was determined not to let that happen. He called my sister, Mariah. He needed her help because I gave him a pretty good fight. He needed her assistance to get me in the van. He needed Mariah to drive so that he could keep me from jumping out. That was exactly what I tried to do as we drove 75mph down the highway.

Will used all of his might to keep me in the van, and my adrenalin allowed me to fight back ten times my normal strength. My goal was to open the van door and jump out as we raced down the road. I forced my way from Will's firm grip and finally made it to the door. It was quite a fight. I reached for the handle and opened it. Mariah screamed and slammed on the brakes. The massive van door slid shut and crushed my leg. I thought my leg was broken, but that was the least of my worries. I had to get away. The van had stopped, and it was the perfect chance to flee. Pain did not faze me, and Will and I wrestled for what seemed like hours.

Suddenly my attention diverted to the sound of ambulance sirens. I was caught off guard, which allowed my husband to get a firm hold on me. It was impossible for me to escape. I knew what Mariah had done. She had called for help. They were going to take me away.

The ambulance pulled up behind our van, and the driver came to see what was going on. I heard Mariah as she explained what had happened. I don't think the EMT crew fathomed the severity of the situation. They did not know what they were in for because all they saw was a skinny sick girl who was giving her husband a little bit of trouble. They didn't know that I was fighting for my life, and I was determined to get away no matter what I had to do.

My next plan to escape could have turned into tragedy, but by the grace of the Lord it didn't. The Lord watched out for me that day because what I was about to do could have destroyed my whole life. If I had followed through with it I would have been placed in an institution for the criminally insane for the rest of my life.

I didn't give the ambulance crew much of a fight at first, and I knew they thought that the trip was going to be easy. With no hurry they crept down the highway at 55 mph. They did not see the situation as an emergency until I turned violent and threatened a crewmember's life.

I told the gentleman, who was in the back of the ambulance with me, that God told me that I had to kill him. I tried to grab for his scissors, but his mighty strong grip prevented me from taking them. Without hesitation the lights and siren were turned on, and the ambulance raced down the road at a lightning speed. I had proved to them that I could be dangerous, and they finally decided to treat the situation as a crisis. It wasn't until I got to the hospital that I had the fight of my life.

The ambulance took me to St. Elizabeth's Hospital in Belleville, Illinois, and when we arrived the police met us. I scratched, kicked, and threw punches. The driver called for the police's assistance to keep me under control. As soon as I arrived the police placed handcuffs on me. I tried so hard to break free that the handcuffs left cuts on my wrists. I refused to do what the police told me because I thought they were taking me away forever. I knew they were in on the plan to take me to hell. I threw myself on the floor and refused to move. Three police officers wrestled with me as I kicked and fought with all of my strength. I felt like I had nothing to lose because if they won I would be consumed by a rage of fire. I was thoroughly convinced that I was going to burn forever. This detrimental threat forced me to push myself beyond my normal strength.

After that strenuous fight with the police I was extremely sore and exhausted. I finally reached a point where I had to give up. I accepted my fate and started to cooperate. I had no choice because the fight weakened me. I was so fatigued that I allowed the nurses to restrain my feet and arms to the bed without a struggle. I was completely distraught as I waited in the emergency room.

The stormy weather added to the dismal day. There were several tornados sighted in the area, which made the scene in the hospital even more chaotic. The electricity went out a few times and the staff members rushed around and tried to get patients to safety. This atmosphere made me even more unsettled and not being able to move made me very hostile. I could feel my stress getting worse. Everyone knew that it was going to be a long and eventful night.

Chapter • Eighteen

Christ's Return

"Give thanks to the Lord, for he is good; his love endures forever.**"**

Psalm 118: 1

"Christ will return! Christ will return!" This is what I chanted to everyone in the emergency room. All heads turned in curiosity, and I could tell that everyone was caught off guard by my abnormal behavior.

I had a vision of the last day. God's voice had returned and had given me insight about when Christ would come back. Suddenly a date appeared on T. V., and I knew that this was a sign. The date was July 8, 2005. I was certain that this was the end even though it was really just a date when a movie, that was just advertised, would be in theaters. It was July 4, 2005 so I was convinced that the world would end in four days.

My family finally walked into the room, and I knew I had to tell them. That was the first thing that I spoke of when they were by my side. They were used to my absurd disposition, and it did not faze them that I had everyone's attention. My mom attempted to comfort me. She reminded me that the Bible states that no one would know the day when Christ will return. I was still convinced that the Lord had given me a sign, and I was the only one that knew the day of his return.

The emergency room was packed that evening, and I waited, restrained to that hospital bed for hours, before a doctor was able to see me. I knew they were going to make me stay, and this was the last thing that I wanted.

"When was I going to be able to see my girls again?" How long was I going to have to stay?" These were the thoughts that overwhelmed my thinking as I tried to hold back my tears. No one gave me an answer to any of these questions, and that frustrated me.

I started to recall my last stay in the hospital and how horrible it was. I could not accept the fact that I was going to have to go through that experience again. The nurses tried to get me to sign the paper work so that I could be admitted to the psychiatric floor. I would not let that happen so I refused to sign myself in. Will warned me that if I didn't then I would be forced to return to the hospital in East St. Louis. Without hesitation I changed my mind. I signed the papers, and I was officially admitted into the hospital for who knew how long. I was devastated.

A room was finally ready for me, and I was wheeled to the psychiatric floor. I was thoroughly perplexed, and I did not know where they were taking me. I panicked because I envisioned the worst, and I was self-assured that I was being taken to my undying doom.

"Take me up! Take me up!" I bellowed when we approached the elevators. I demanded that they take me up. In my mind going down meant intense heat for eternity, and up meant perfect peaceful paradise.

To my relief we ascended to the top floor. At that moment I suddenly relaxed because I was being taken to heaven. When we got to the psychiatric floor I was thoroughly disappointed because it was far from what I imagined heaven would be. A few patients yelled, groaned and complained. It seemed like complete chaos that I did not want to be a part of. To my displeasure I had no choice, and I had absolutely no idea when I would return home. My surroundings troubled me, and I felt very uneasy.

"How long would I survive in here?" I thought to myself. I was trapped without any sign of being released.

Chapter • Nineteen

....

Fireworks

❝Your sun will never set again, and your moon will
wane no more; the Lord will be your <u>everlasting</u> light,
and your days of sorrow will end. **❞**

Isaiah 60:20

The fascinating multicolored glow filled the sky
and lit up my hospital room like a Christmas
tree. The aesthetic fireworks sparkled outside
my hospital room window. Even though they
were gorgeous they filled me with discourage-
ment because I wanted to watch them with my
family.

It was July 4, and normally I celebrated the
holiday eating barbeque, swimming in our pool,
and playing volleyball with friends and relatives.
Lying in bed by myself disheartened me, and it
weakened my spirits. I wondered what my family
was doing, and I longed to be with them.

"I should have set them all on fire and
watched them burn!"

My thoughts were startled by this disturbing comment. My curiosity forced me out of bed to see who yelled this unsettling remark. A very crude looking man continued to chant this. His tattooed body, straggly long hair and the evil glow in his eyes horrified me. I instantly thought that this comment was directed toward me, and I was devastated. This devilish man was after me and I had to hide. I ran to my bed and tried to comfort myself. I closed my eyes and hoped that sleep would take me away from this living nightmare. Sleep was not possible, and I had to listen to this man's taunting words. After what seemed like forever the racket stopped, but I still did not think clearly. I feared that he would find me and watch me burn. I dreaded these thoughts, and it kept me from sleep.

I refused to get out of bed the next morning because I feared that that horrid man would find me. A nurse stepped in my room, and politely told me that it was breakfast time. I did not get up, and I missed breakfast. At least I was safe in my own room. The activity director came to my room and encouraged me to get out of bed to make some crafts. I told her no thank you, but she replied and said, "You are never going to get better by lying in bed." I did not want to leave the comfort of my own room. I stayed in my own bed for most of the morning, but I did not get away with this for very long. At the call for lunch I was commanded to get up and eat. I had not drunk or ate anything, and the staff was concerned with this behavior. I finally got out of bed, but I was scared for my life. I cautiously crept to the hall and thoroughly looked it over for any signs of my predator. When I was absolutely sure that the hall was cleared I grabbed my lunch and timidly went to the dining room. I scanned the room, and it was clear from danger. No one said a word to me, and I felt alone as I picked through my nutritious but very bland lunch. I never saw that crude mysterious man again.

Chapter • Twenty

Misinterpretations

"Why are you downcast, O my soul? Why so
disturbed within me? Put your hope in God, for I will
yet praise him my Savior.**"**

Psalm 42:5

After lunch I felt very strange again. Nonsensical
thoughts tormented me throughout the first day.
I misinterpreted the small petty situations that
had logical explanations. I made these events
into something they were not.

All the rooms on one side of the hall were
cold, and the other rooms, which included mine,
were very warm. The reason for this was that the
air conditioning did not work on my side of the
hall. I construed this to be that my side of the hall
would be sent to hell, and the other side would
be sent to heaven. I assumed the nurses turned
off the air conditioning to get those that were
lost and would suffer the fiery pit forever use to
the hot temperatures. I comforted myself with
the thought that if I could get my bed moved

over to the other side of the hall I would go to heaven, too. The next two days I focused all my energy into convincing the staff that I needed to move over to the other side of the hall. I put my heart and soul into getting myself moved, but I was unsuccessful. This made me stressed.

I looked for other options to either get to heaven or escape the entrapment of the hospital. I convinced myself that there had to be a secret door that would lead me outside. As if I were playing a scavenger hunt I intently searched my room for the passageway. I was confident that I found it when I went to the bathroom and saw the emergency call switch. With excitement I pulled on it with all my strength, and I broke it. A secret door was not revealed, and I was disappointed. Feeling ashamed I took the broken switch to a nurse. The nurse asked no questions, but from the disgusted look on her face I knew she was frustrated.

The television in the dining area was broke. Only half the screen would show. I was truly convinced that God was taking my eyesight, and I was gradually being blinded. No one could change my mind about this even though the nurses reassured me that my eyesight was perfectly fine. I avoided watching T.V. because I feared the worst.

A mysterious female patient, who was not coherent, wondered around the hospital as if she were lost. I started to become her shadow when I realized her room was on heaven's side of the hall. I wanted the nurses to see that we were friends. I hoped that they saw it would be to her benefit to have a good friend room with her. I wanted to get to her side of the hall. I followed her everywhere and sat next to her when we ate. One day I did something that was strictly prohibited. I followed her into her room, and I was warned not to follow her around anymore. My plan had failed.

There was a phone at the end of the hall. I was anxious to use it. I wanted to hear my husband's voice, and I was curious to know how my girls were doing. I envied the patients who talked to their loved ones. I longed to do the same. One day

I curiously wondered to the phone to call home. It took me a few minutes to recall my phone number. After I sat and contemplated for a while I finally remembered. I was excited as I dialed my number. My stomach turned with excitement as I pressed the last number. If I could hear the precious sound of Hannah's and Adrianna's voice my day would be perfect. As I anticipated it to start ringing I was completely disappointed when a loud busy signal discouraged my positive thoughts. Determined, I tried again and again. The more I tried the harder I pressed the buttons. Each time I got more frustrated, and I started to cry. I was disappointed again which added to my depression. I construed another ridiculous interpretation that the nurses kept me from talking to my family. They were against me and turned the phones off when I tried to use it. I was furious and extremely hopeless. The nurses hated me and wanted to watch me suffer. They had managed to keep me on hell's side of the hall without any contact with my loved ones. I wanted to die, but I wanted someone else to kill me.

Chapter • Twenty One

Recruiting My Killer

The hospital made me more insane. The other patients influenced me, and I felt worse. I needed to get out of that horrid place. One afternoon I tried to escape. I nonchalantly walked toward the securely locked door. I punched in random numbers. Then I punched in my phone number, my room number, and my social security number. Obviously these numbers would not work, but my thoughts were so distorted I was desperate and tried anything. My plan failed again.

I had hit bottom, and all hope was gone. I needed someone to end my life. I started to talk with a very nice patient. She seemed very pleasant, and I really needed a friend. She told me about her life and why she was in the hospital. I told her about myself.

One night I asked her to kill me in my sleep. I told her to come into my room in the middle of the night and end my life.

"I can't do that!" she replied with great concern.

Looking back I realized how dangerous that request was. I was asking a total stranger who was a patient on a psychiatric floor to kill me. Considering the circumstances there was a good chance that the request could have been fulfilled. I feel strongly that the Lord protected me from danger that night. It was by his grace that I asked a sweet patient who was not insane enough to fulfill that request. To this day she has become a good friend. We write to each other for encouragement and support. The Lord blessed me with a wonderful friend.

The only way I was going to escape my nightmare was by killing myself. I had planned to jump from my hospital room window. My only question was, how was I going to get the window open? I pushed as hard as I could, but the window would not budge. I knew I had to break it. With all my strength I closed my hand into a tight fist. I tightened it so much that I felt my hand go numb. With a mighty force I punched the glass window as hard as I could. I stopped and realized that I didn't do anything. I wanted to break the window so bad I punched it three times as fast as I could. The only thing I did was made my knuckles bleed. My hand ached so bad that I decided to give up. I walked to the bathroom and washed my bloody hand. I wept because another plan had failed.

Another ridiculous plan filled my head. I decided to pray to God to end my life and to do it soon. I could not stand another minute of living in this deranged hospital. I was so delusional that I did not care that I would be headed for hell if I died. Depression had forced me to ask my creator to annihilate me.

After I prayed I was waiting for my life to end. I wondered how God was going to end it. A few days had passed and I was still alive. I decided that he was not going to answer my prayer, and then I started experiencing falling spells. I was not eating or drinking very much, and this obviously debilitated me. When I would stand or walk around for very long I would get light headed and fall to the ground. My insane mind translated this to be that the Lord was trying to murder me, but I was so stubborn that I was not dying. The medical explanation for these falling spells was dehydration and extreme weakness.

I remember one day when my preacher, Jim Stark, came to visit me. I was having these falling spells, and I explained to him that I had asked God to kill me. I told Jim that he was trying to kill me, but I would not die. He told me that if God wanted me die I would die. Jim reminded me that he is the almighty creator and has power over everything even my demise. On his visit Jim also inspired me with a hymn called, "O Love that Will Not Let Me Go," by George Matheson, who wrote this song while experiencing his mental anguish. At that point I did not understand what this hymn meant and was not aware that its life-altering message would be the inspiration of my testimony and the reason for my book. After praying with Jim and listening to God's word I realized that God was in control and would kill me if he wanted me dead. Slowly my thinking started to become clearer, and I knew Jim's words were the beginning of God's plan for my recovery.

Chapter • Twenty Two

A Slow and Successful Recovery

66 If we are faithless he will remain faithful, for he cannot disown himself. **99**

2 Timothy 2:13

I had forgotten how wonderful a simple smile and some laughter could be until I finally laughed for the first time in two months. I took something as small as this for granted until it was taken away, and I realized how important it was to my happiness and quality of life. That was the first time I knew I was getting better when I was so caught up in my laughter that I forgot about my problems. Laughing seemed strange to me because I had not done this in a long time, but it felt very good. Praise the Lord for laughter!

The reason for that happy occasion was a visit from my mom, dad and Will. I finally felt well enough to play cards and to enjoy my family as they visited. They told me funny stories about Hannah and Adrianna that brought a smile to my face. My eyes met my husband's, and I instantly knew that he felt the same way I did about that unforgettable smile that filled my face. When I was lost in his eyes and saw a smile cover his face we both knew that I was on the road to recovery. That visit was a blessing from the Lord, and for the first time I seen a glimpse of hope. I could not believe that just the day before I wanted to die. I could not comprehend how I could have felt this way when I had two precious children at home who wanted to see their mother again.

My life at the hospital changed after that night of playing cards. I realized that everyone at church, my friends and family had been praying for me. I started to see the miraculous power of prayer being answered. God kept steering my thoughts to the hymn that Jim gave me. I thought deeply about the title, "The Love That Will Not Let Me Go." The Lord opened my eyes to its message and the fact that I am God's child forever. He will never leave me, and he will always forgive me. It is in God's time and his time is perfect. Even though I was getting impatient, and I wanted an answer quickly I realized that the Lord has a plan for everything and his plan is faultless.

The beginning of my recovery was obvious when I started waking up feeling refreshed with a smile on my face. I was anxious to start the day, and I had more energy than ever before. I attended the craft classes and the counseling sessions. The nurses started to notice these improvements, and I started realizing that they were my friends. I wanted to go home, but it was not because I was mad or dissatisfied. It was because I was thinking clearer and I felt like I was ready.

One day I was given some extraordinary news. My nurse told me that she was amazed at how well I was recovering, and the doctor had decided to move me to another hall. This hall was for patients who were close to going home. This filled me with joy and I was eager to move.

I had been at the hospital for nine days and on the tenth day I was told that I was headed home. When my husband came to my hospital room door I engulfed him with a hug. This was the moment that I had waited for. I visualized hugging my girls and kissing their cheeks.

Meeting my children for the first time with a clear mind was simply amazing. They ran to me with open arms and the sweet sound of them yelling my name brought cheerful tears to my eyes. I wanted to hug them and not let go. Even though I had a long way to go to understand the lessons that God wanted me to learn from this personal awakening it was a great start to a tremendous life of freedom.

Chapter • Twenty Three

The Lord Sets Me Free

❝In my anguish I cried to the Lord, and he answered by setting me free.**❞**

Psalm 118:5

There were some hardships after returning home. I was diagnosed with Bipolar Depression, and my doctor warned me that it could happen again. He gave me some peace of mind by telling me that if the medicine was the correct medicine for me then it would not happen as long as I took my prescription. I still worried that my mental illness was going to rudely interrupt my life again, but to this day I have to trust that the Lord will love and take care of me. I have learned to put the situation in his hands.

At first I was embarrassed of my mental illness, but the Lord has made me realize that I did not ask for this disease. It's the same as a cancer patient or a patient with heart disease who has not asked for the condition that they have. I am an innocent patient that did not do anything to cause my mental disease. With the Lord's help I actually see this illness as my opportunity to spread my testimony and to do the Lord's work by helping others who struggle with the same disease or their assurance of heaven. I am confident that the Lord will use my experience to bring those that are lost and Christians who are confused closer to him. With this thought I know I have been blessed with this disease to do God's work. This is why I am eager to take on any future personal awakening that God has in store for me.

I am still taking the same medicine that I left the hospital with that summer day back in 2005. Despite some of the medication nightmares that I have heard with other patients with the same mental condition, I haven't had to change or experiment with any other prescription. I have heard about patients who have the same condition who are not functional, and I am highly functional. This is a definite answer to prayer. A doctor also told Will that I would never be the same again. In a sense he was right because I have never felt better in all my life, and by God's grace I trust that my happiness and confidence is going to continue to improve.

It has been almost five years since that horrible life altering experience, but I would not have had it any other way. God has led me on an enlightening and astounding five-year road to recovery. He has taught me some amazing lessons about life and my personal walk with him. He has freed me from my anguish and my hopelessness of heaven. I am happier and more confident as a Christian, mother, and teacher. During these years after my hospitalization the Lord graciously helped me get through Graduate School. I have successfully earned my Master's Degree. God has taught me what it means to fear him and him alone. Life has become easier to live because I have a clear mind and a stronger relationship with my heavenly father. Now, I read that hymn, "O Love That Will Not Let Me Go" with confidence that God's love is eternal and will never leave me. I now understand that

I only had to ask the Lord into my life once and I am his for eternal life. I have a place in heaven reserved just for me, and that gives me hope and motivation to serve him. I now realize that I am not perfect, and I will continue to sin until my heavenly father takes me home. I now have the assurance that when my life is over I will rejoice in heaven for eternal life. I pray that by reading my personal awakening that it will also be yours and that I will be able to rejoice in heaven with you forever, too.

We love Mexico! After a refreshing day relaxing in the pool, and lying in the sun we are now ready for dinner. I can now enjoy and relax on our family vacations. My worries are in God's hands now.

My precious girls always fill me with joy. Hannah, my oldest, is shy, but she is very good at softball. She is my star pitcher. Adrianna is very energetic and talkative. She started reading before Kindergarten and she still loves to read.

Adrianna and I enjoy another evening in Mexico. We are posing in our room patiently waiting for everyone to get ready for dinner. This is our favorite vacation spot. I thank the Lord for another wonderful day with my family.

Will and I get a vacation by ourselves. Dinner is over and we are waiting for the evening show to start. At the show we were chosen to play a game on stage. It was very fun and entertaining.

Our Mexican resorts are always extraordinary. Will and I love strolling around the resort in the evening taking pictures and enjoying the peaceful scenary.

Epilogue

The bright beautiful morning sun shines through my window as the cheerful birds sing. The sun seems to shine brighter, and the birds are more peaceful. A new day starts as I stretch and eagerly get out of bed. A huge smile covers my face. The Lord blesses me with another wonderful night's sleep. I feel refreshed and ready to conquer a day with my students and my children. I know it is going to be a good day because I am a child of God, and I am living for him and him alone. My days are easier and full of satisfaction now that my eyes have been opened, and I have a clear understanding of my life as a Christian.

I am full of energy as I wake my girls up for another day of school. Showers are taken and breakfast is made. The small tasks seem easier and more rewarding as I feel blessed to be alive and well. Hugs and kisses are lovingly given as I put Hannah and Adrianna on the bus. I am anxious to start my day because the Lord has freed me from my shackles. Stress is not a problem anymore.

I walk into my classroom with a cheerful heart and a positive attitude. I take each day a day at a time knowing that what I don't get done today will get done tomorrow. I take into consideration that all students learn differently and at a different pace. God has made me realize that it is not my fault if a child misbehaves or if they just don't get the math lesson for the day. It takes practice and time for some students to master a skill or to change their behavior. I can only do the best I can and not fret over what I can't control. I now know that my students come from different environments and are influenced by negative attitudes at home, and these are the circumstances that I have no control over. I have put the Lord in the driver's seat so that I can seek him for the assurance and confidence I need each day.

The first bell rings, and I happily greet every student with a smile as they walk into my classroom. I am full of life and ready to teach to glorify and please the Lord. I have a new goal and outlook which allows me to enjoy my job and be an effective teacher. I will make mistakes, but I will learn from them and they will make me a better person.

After a day at school I am not exhausted and overwhelmed. I put my day at school behind me and I do not let it affect the way I relate to my family at home. I am excited to see my precious girls and my loving husband. If Will or my girls are in foul moods I know it is not my fault, and I try to remain patient. I enjoy the evenings relaxing with my family, and I am flexible with getting my papers graded. If I feel that I need to help my children or enjoy a movie with my husband then my homework can wait. It will be there tomorrow.

Vacations are much more enjoyable with my new perspective and outlook on life. I take the time to enjoy the little things in life like sitting on the porch and letting the refreshing breeze gently blow through my hair.

People do not control me anymore because I am not living to please them but to please my Lord in heaven. I am more confident with others, and I am willing and even eager now to start a conversation with anyone. I use to avoid others for fear of making a mistake or what they might think of me. This does not matter to me anymore because I am accepted by God, and that is all that counts. I am a child of God and I am headed for heaven for eternal life, and that is what makes me rejoice every day. I feel confident that the Lord will use me to help others to turn from their troubles and seek them. This gives me the motivation and purpose to live and love others as the Lord loves me. I know now that the Lord has a love that will never let me go.

"O Love That Will Not Let Me Go"

By, George Matheson

1. O Love that will not let me go,
   I rest my weary soul in thee;
   I give thee back the life I owe,
   That in thine ocean depths its flow
   May richer, fuller be.

2. O light that followest all my way,
   I yield my flickering torch to thee;
   My heart restores its borrowed ray,
   That in thy sunshine's blaze its day
   May brighter, fairer be.

3. O Joy that sleekest me through pain,
   I cannot close my heart to thee;
   I trace the rainbow through the rain,
   And feel the promise is not vain,
   That morn shall tearless be.

4. O Cross that liftest up my head,
   I dare not ask to fly from thee;

I lay in dust life's glory dead,
And from the ground there blossoms red
Life that shall endless be.

Made in USA - Kendallville, IN
1226495_9781452884516
01.20.2021 0742